This book belongs to

....

....

Meet the Large family

Mr Large

Mr Large does his best to help out around the house and manages to stay calm amid the chaos created by his boisterous children.

Lester Large

Nine-year-old Lester just wants to look cool and play on his skateboard. He loves his family, but often finds them a bit embarrassing.

Luke Large

Luke is cheerful and sometimes shy. He looks up to his cool older brother Lester, but still enjoys playing with his toys, especially his old favourite, Mr Teddy.

Mrs Large

Mrs Large is always in a rush as she struggles to cope with her four children and mountains of washing. But she always has time to join in the fun!

Laura Large

Helpful and good-natured, Laura is a caring big sister to baby Lucy. She is creative and practical and enjoys making things.

Lucy Large

Lucy is the baby of the family. She gets into mischief the moment Mrs Large turns her back and her naughty little trunk finds its way into everything.

First published 2008 by Walker Books Ltd
87 Vauxhall Walk, London SE11 5HJ

2 4 6 8 10 9 7 5 3 1

This book has been typeset in Bembo Educational.

Printed in China

British Library Cataloguing in Publication Data: a catalogue record for this book
is available from the British Library

ISBN 978-1-4063-1474-8

www.walkerbooks.co.uk

Lucy Meets
Mr Chilly

Based on the Large Family stories by Jill Murphy

WALKER BOOKS

AND SUBSIDIARIES

LONDON · BOSTON · SYDNEY · AUCKLAND

"Look what's outside!" cried Mr Large,
as he opened the kitchen curtains.

"SNOW!" yelled the children, rushing for the door.

"Coats on first!" called Mrs Large.

"Make way for the snow slider!" yelled Luke,
as he slid across the garden on his toboggan.

"Think that's cool?" yelled Lester. "Watch this! Fly like a bird!" He flew through the air on his skateboard and landed flat on his back. "And land like an elephant!" laughed Laura.

Mr Large started to make a snow elephant.
"Over here, boys!" he called. "How about
lending a hand?"
"Oh, Da–ad!" said Lester. "Snow elephants
are *so* yesterday."

"How's this for a little more today?" chuckled
Mr Large, throwing a snowball at Lester.

"Lucy," called Mr Large. "Come and meet our frosty friend."

"Nice one, Dad!" said Lester. "He's cool!"

"No, he isn't!" laughed Laura. "He's chilly – say hello to Mr Chilly, Lucy."

Lucy squealed with delight when she saw
Mr Chilly, showing him her toys and doing
a little dance.

Laura was caught in the middle of a snowball fight between Lester and Luke.

Meanwhile, Lucy was busy dressing Mr Chilly
with a scarf-belt around his waist.

Mrs Large appeared at the door with hot
chocolate for everyone, just as a dollop
of snow slid off the roof!

Mrs Large looked up at the sky. "The sun's coming out," she said. "Things will start melting soon."

"Melting!" cried Laura. "Oh, no! What will happen to Mr Chilly?"
"He'll melt too," said Mrs Large, "and poor Lucy will be heartbroken."

"We've got to do something fast," said Lester,
"before Mr Chilly turns into a giant puddle."

Lester and Laura rushed to the garage and found a large sunshade, while Luke grabbed some ice and frozen vegetables from the freezer.

They set up the sunshade above Mr Chilly
and tucked the ice and vegetables into the
scarf around his waist.

But it was no use, Mr Chilly was already melting. "Poor Chilly," said Lucy, starting to cry.

"Don't worry, Lucy," said Luke. "I'm sure we'll think of something."
"And I know just what that something is!" exclaimed Lester.

Lester ran into the house and found some old
white socks, while Luke pulled a little red hat
from his toy box. Laura took everything to
her mum and Mrs Large started to sew.

Lucy was hanging onto the melting Mr Chilly
when Lester arrived with the toy they had
all made.
"Look, Lucy," he said, holding the little snow
elephant out to her. "Baby Chilly's come to
be your new friend."

Lucy was thrilled and gave Baby Chilly
a big hug.
"I think she likes it!" said Laura
with a smile.

"Good thinking, Lester!" said Mr Large. "You saved the day!"

"So did I!" said Laura. "I helped!"

"And me!" said Luke.

"All of you," said Mr Large, proudly.

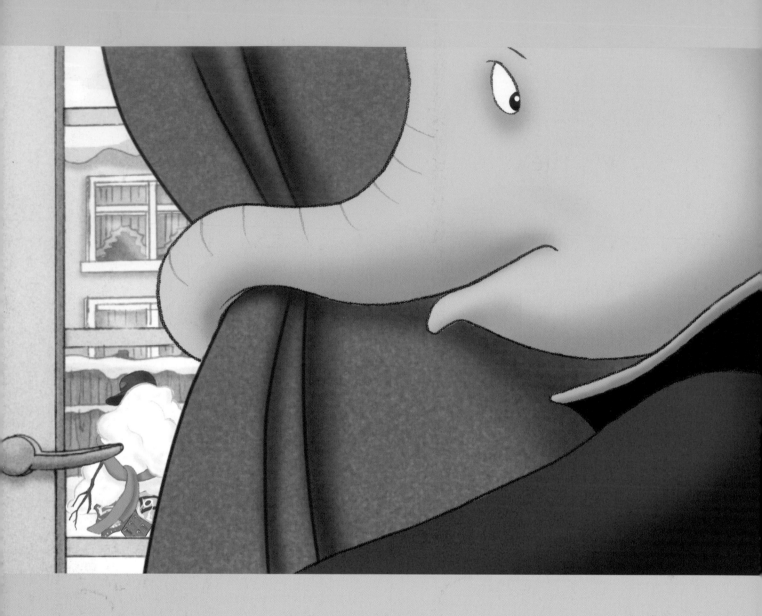

Mrs Large went to pull the curtains shut in the living room in case the melting scene outside upset Lucy.

But Lucy surprised everyone by happily waving
goodbye to the melting Mr Chilly.
She and Baby Chilly waved goodbye together.
"Bye-bye, Mr Chilly," said Lucy. "See you
again soon."